The Ancient Mariner

Written by Sue Purkiss
Illustrated by Amerigo Pinelli

Collins

I stared at the old man. Who was he? I'd never seen him before; I was sure of it. I'd have remembered if I had. He had a long grey beard and scruffy clothes – but his eyes were the strangest thing about him. Once you'd seen them, you wouldn't forget them in a hurry, no matter how much you wanted to. They glittered as they stared at me, with a piercing, merciless gaze, and I found that, no matter how hard I tried, I couldn't look away.

I suppose my friends thought I knew him. Anyway, they were impatient to get to the wedding – we were nearly there, we could hear the music and the voices – and they carried on without me. Thanks a lot, I thought. Then the old man spoke.

"There was a ship," he began.

Suddenly, I felt angry. I wanted to go to the wedding, and I didn't want anything to do with him. Whatever his problem was, it was nothing to do with me. I told him to get out of the way. But he placed his hand on my chest, and he said it again.

"There was a ship …"

And, as if in a dream, I found myself sitting down on a nearby stone. It seemed I'd no choice but to listen, as he went on to tell me his story – the story of the Ancient Mariner.

Chapter 1

There was a ship. I was one of the crew. We were setting off to explore the seas around the South Pole – it was going to be a great adventure.

All our friends and relatives came to see us off, and they waved as we left the harbour.

As we sailed south, the sun climbed higher and the sky was
a perfect blue. But as we went on, the weather began to change.
Black clouds raced across the sky and a strong wind got up.
It lashed the waves till they were as high as the ship, and we had
to cling on to the masts or whatever we could so we wouldn't be
washed overboard. We were driven before the storm like a twig
caught by a river in flood.

We were sure the ship would break up and sink, but at long last the gale died down. Now, however, we had a new problem. It grew cold – bitterly, fiercely cold. The ship drifted through mist and snow. Our breath came out in clouds and our eyebrows and beards were crusted with ice. We put on all the clothes we had and they still weren't enough. We didn't see a single living thing, neither in the sea nor in the air.

It was beautiful, though, no denying that. Massive icebergs drifted past – great cliffs and mountains of ice. They shone with blue and green fire, but of course it was a cold fire that wouldn't warm us.

8

Then one day I looked over the side and noticed that something new was happening. Patches of ice were floating on the surface. Surely the sea itself couldn't freeze? At first they were quite small, but they grew bigger – and bigger – and bigger. All of us gathered at the railing and watched. We talked about what we were seeing, but gradually we fell silent. I could see in all the other sailors' faces that they were afraid of the same thing as I was.

As the temperature dropped, the pieces of ice were joining together, like a jigsaw. Soon, they'd form one vast sheet.

With no wind to fill the sails, the ship couldn't turn back.

We wouldn't be able to move.

The ship would be seized fast, and what would happen to us then?

It went on for days. At first, the ice was quite a thin layer, but it grew thicker, and thicker, and thicker. Then the sounds began – great slabs of ice grinding against each other. The ice creaked and howled and groaned. It sounded like a living being, a creature in pain.

But it wasn't in as much pain as we were. Our supplies were getting low. Our drinking water froze. We had frostbite in our fingers and toes. Then one man said what we were all thinking.

"If the ice keeps getting thicker, in the end, it'll crush the ship."

We stared at each other in dread.

How could we escape? What could we do?

The answer seemed to be – *nothing*. We were helpless.

And then, after several terrible days of being caught in the grip of the ice, I happened to look up, and saw a tiny dot in the sky. It came closer – it was a bird! In this frozen wilderness, something was alive!

It circled above the ship on huge wings, and we all gazed at it, thrilled. It was an albatross. It dipped down, as if to take a closer look at us, and someone had the bright idea of getting some biscuit to lure it closer. The biscuit was stale, but the bird didn't mind – it seemed to think it was a great treat. After that, it kept close to us and came at our call.

Well, it was as if this beautiful bird had brought us luck. A couple of days after we first saw it, there was a cracking sound beneath the ship and the ice sheet split. A south wind blew up and filled our sails, and carefully, we nosed our way out through the channels that had appeared in the ice. It looked as though after all, thanks to the albatross, we were going to escape.

And so … what made me do it? How can I explain it? Was there some evil inside me? Was I just stupid? Had I forgotten that we owed all our luck to the bird?

I don't know. All I know is that in a single, terrible, stupid moment – I raised my crossbow and I shot the albatross.

Chapter 2

I can see the faces of the crew now. They looked at me in absolute horror. Even my own nephew, who was on the ship with me. The bird had brought us luck, we all knew that – without its help we'd never have escaped the ice. None of them could believe what I'd done and neither could I.
I began to tremble. I fell to my knees. What had I been thinking? True, at home, in the countryside, I used to go out and shoot birds for the pot – but this was no ordinary bird and I knew that as well as anyone.

The sun was still shining, the wind was still there, but no bird followed or came when we called. Everyone was strung-up and tense, certain that bad luck was bound to follow.

But then … the sun still shone, and the breeze still blew, and they began to change their tune. Perhaps they'd got it wrong, someone suggested. Perhaps the bird had actually caused the fog and snow.

But it was a false hope. As we sailed north, it got warmer. The breeze drop, and the sails did too. Soon, the sun was pitiless, scorching hot in a blazing sky. Day after day, the ship drifted, a tiny speck in a huge ocean. We were surrounded by water, but before long we didn't have a drop to drink. Our mouths were dry, our lips were cracked. We grew weaker and weaker. We began to despair.

At night, strange lights flashed across the sky, blue and green and white. Our sleep was broken by nightmares. Several dreamt of a spirit, a phantom. They said it had followed us from the land of mist and snow. We couldn't see it, but it was there, deep beneath the ocean, and it was determined to punish us – for the thing that I alone had done.

Eventually, our throats became so dry we could no longer speak. But that didn't stop their burning eyes from glaring at me. And it didn't stop them hanging the body of the albatross round my neck, to remind me of what I'd done.

As if I could ever forget!

Then, one day, as I gazed drearily out to sea, I saw a black speck. I thought I was imagining things. It seemed to twist and turn and duck and dive. At first, I couldn't make out what it was. Then, as it came closer …

Somehow, I managed to speak. I pointed, and croaked, "Look! A sail! A sail!" Their faces lit up, and we all watched eagerly as the ship drew closer.

It was evening, and the sea glowed like fire in the west. We waited impatiently, hope bubbling up inside of us.

But I began to see that there was something strange about this ship.
It was moving too fast, for one thing. We were drifting – why wasn't
this ship? And its sails – they were tattered, like spiders' webs.
Any wind would just blow straight through them.

The ship drove in front of the red sun. Its masts were black and
splintered. A feeling of dread began to creep over me.
What kind of a ship was this?

It got even worse. Soon, the ship was close enough for us to see its crew.

There were only two people on the deck, and they were both hideous.

One was a skeleton. The other was a woman. She was beautiful, and yet there was something about her that made her even more frightening than the skeleton. Her lips were too red, her skin was too white … One glance at her, and my heart sank. I didn't dare to look at my companions. I'd caused their hopes to rise, but yet again, I'd dashed them.

The wreck shouldn't have even been able to float. But it came alongside us all the same, so close we could see that these two unnatural figures were playing a game of dice. All at once, the woman cried out, "That's it, the game's over! I've won, I've won!" She looked across at us and cackled in triumph.

I knew then that something awful was going to happen.

It did.

A sudden gust of wind blew up out of nowhere, rattling the bones of the skeleton. The black ship sailed off at an unnatural speed, and before long, it had disappeared. I could still hear that horrible laughter. Then all 200 of the crew turned towards me. They gazed at me sadly, their eyes glittering in the pale light of the moon.

Then they fell down on to the deck, one by one.

Lifeless.

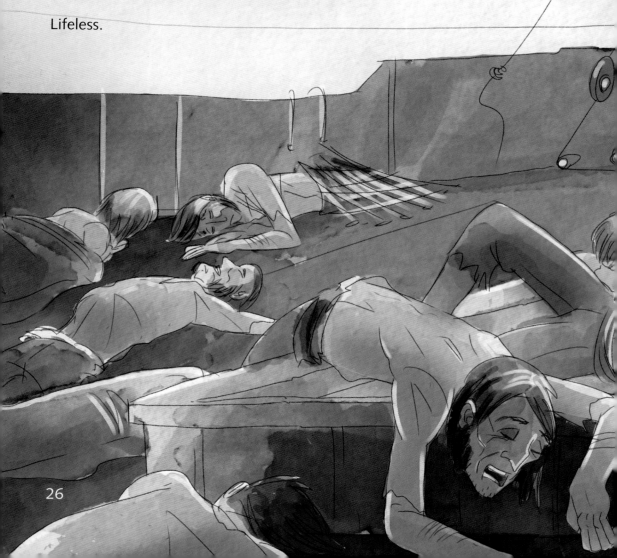

Chapter 3

I stared at the Ancient Mariner. I don't mind admitting it, I was terrified. The whole crew had dropped dead, he'd said. What about him?

He knew what I was thinking. He laughed, but it was a bitter sound. "Oh, don't worry. I didn't die. I'm not a ghost. The others all fell, but not me. So there I was. The only soul left on the ship, and as far as I could tell, the only thing alive on that entire ocean ..."

Can you imagine how guilty I felt? I was alive, and yet I was the one who'd shot the albatross – it was all my fault. I was filled with disgust. It seemed to me that everything around me was disgusting too. I looked at the sea, and saw no hope there. I looked at the burning sky, and saw no hope there either. But if I looked at the deck of the ship – why, that was worst of all. Because they all lay there, looking just as they had at the moment they'd died. All their eyes accused me still.

For seven days and seven nights, this carried on. I don't know why I didn't die too. I was desperately hungry, desperately thirsty – but worst of all, I knew I'd only myself to blame. And the dead crew's eyes told me that they agreed.

But then, on the seventh night, the moon rose. It was a beautiful night. The sky was sprinkled with stars, and the moonlight made a silver path across the ocean. The sea rippled and sighed, always restless, never still. Something caught my eye in the water below. I could see fish swimming.

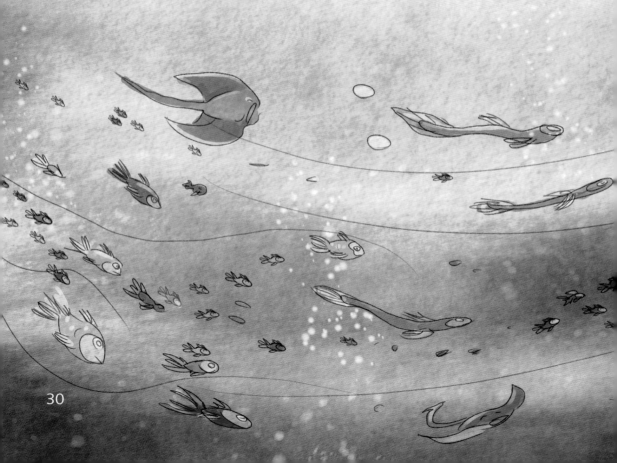

At home, we went out and caught fish to eat, and they were mostly silver or brown. But these – well, I'd never seen such colours! They were turquoise, and glossy green, and bright scarlet, and brilliant yellow, and sapphire blue. And the shapes! Some of them were flat, some were round, some were slender – others were like eels or snakes. They darted about so fast and with such grace – once I saw hundreds of tiny fish, all swimming close together in a mass, twisting and turning like a flock of birds in the sky.

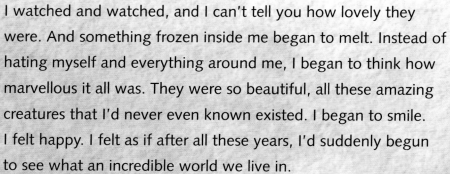

I watched and watched, and I can't tell you how lovely they were. And something frozen inside me began to melt. Instead of hating myself and everything around me, I began to think how marvellous it all was. They were so beautiful, all these amazing creatures that I'd never even known existed. I began to smile. I felt happy. I felt as if after all these years, I'd suddenly begun to see what an incredible world we live in.

And as I thought this, the albatross suddenly fell from my neck, where it had been ever since my ship-mates had fastened it there. It dropped over the side, and sank into the sea like a stone.

I was free!

Chapter 4

That night I slept like a baby. And when I woke up – well!
For so long, as soon as I'd woken up, it had been to a dawn
without hope. Every day, I'd known despair and guilt.

But this day was quite the opposite. In my dreams, the buckets
on deck were filled with water. And when I opened my eyes,
I saw that it was true. In the night, it had rained. I was wet
through – and it was the most marvellous feeling. I felt so
light I thought I could have floated. I drank and drank –
and then I stopped, and listened.

I could hear a sound. It was a roaring sound, like the noise a great waterfall makes when it crashes down into the river below.

Wind! Wind to fill the sails!

But this was no ordinary wind. It rushed towards the ship like a tornado, and then it dropped down like a stone. And as it hit the deck – I hardly know how to tell you this. I couldn't believe it myself, and I saw it with my own eyes.

What happened was this. There was a sound. It wasn't
the wind, it was a groan. And it came from the dead
men. Yes, as sure as I'm standing here, I'm telling you:
those dead men groaned.

And then they stood up.

The helmsman went to the wheel, the sailors went to the ropes. My nephew took his place beside me, just as he always used to. No one spoke, but they all set to and sailed the ship. When the sun rose in the sky, they began to sing. And then a skylark joined in – and a blackbird, and a robin, and then every other kind of bird you can think of. It was like the loveliest music I'd ever heard.

Eventually it stopped, but then the sails made a sound of their own. It was like the noise a fast stream makes, when it flows over stones. And yet now, there was no wind.

The sailors never spoke. I don't think they could even see me. Can you imagine anything more strange? And yet I wasn't afraid. Somehow, I knew that the spirit that had followed us from the land of ice and snow was still with us – but now it was helping me. It was underneath the ship, and it was pushing it along.

Suddenly, the ship sort of bucked. Then it bounded forward, moving much faster than any ordinary ship could move. I think I must've fainted then. In my dreams, I heard a voice say, "Is this the man who shot the albatross?"

And then another, gentler voice said, "It is. But he's sorry for what he's done. He's been punished for it, and his punishment isn't ended yet … but it's time for him to go home now."

Chapter 5

When I woke up, it was night time again. The sea was calm and
the moon was high. The men were still sailing the ship. At first
I was a little afraid, but then a gentle breeze stroked my face and
ruffled my hair, and somehow I knew that everything was going
to be all right. The ship flew along, and the sweet breeze still blew.

At last I saw a dark smudge on the horizon – land! I wondered where I was – though to be honest, I didn't care, so long as I could once again feel solid ground beneath my feet.

But slowly, I realised that the coastline was beginning to look familiar. Could it be – could it possibly be?

Yes!

There was the hill, there was the lighthouse, there was the town – I was home!

I'm not ashamed to admit it – as we came towards the harbour, tears of relief and happiness were running down my cheeks. I couldn't believe that not only had I survived, but that my friends had brought me safely home.

I turned to face them. Their faces were pale, their eyes glittered in the bright moonlight. Each of them raised his arm, and I raised mine in return. It was almost over.

Then I heard the sound of oars. It was the pilot, who comes out with his son to guide ships between the sandbars into the safety of the harbour. As the boat drew nearer, I could see the pilot's expression. He looked puzzled. I had to smile. It was hardly surprising. The sails hung in ruins. Barnacles and seaweed encrusted the hull. One of the masts had broken off and only a splintered section of it remained.

And then, of course, there were my friends …

I thought I was safe – but it turned out that it wasn't over yet. As the pilot's boat came closer, I saw the puzzlement on his face turn to alarm. The calm water was suddenly ruffled, and his boat had begun to rock wildly. Then I heard a sound – it was like thunder, roaring from one side of the bay to the other. But this thunder didn't come from the sky. It came from the sea.

I looked round wildly.

What new horror was this?

The noise grew louder and louder. I was almost deafened. I clapped my hands to my ears. The ship rocked from side to side – then it began to tilt. There was a fearful sucking sound as with terrible speed, the ship began to slide beneath the waves.

I found myself floating on the water – I'd been thrown free. But I still wasn't safe, oh no – because where the ship had vanished, the water was in turmoil. There was a whirlpool. The water swirled round with sickening force and it was doing its level best to suck me under.

But then I spotted the pilot's boat. I managed to swim over to it – thank goodness it wasn't far away, because I hadn't the strength to swim far. I grasped the side of the boat and heaved myself into it.

Then I lay on the bottom, gasping.

The pilot's son looked at me with terrified eyes, and shrank as far away from me as he could.

"Is he a ghost, Father?" he whispered. "Are we going to die?"

I was startled, but then I realised what I must look like. I hadn't had a wash for months. I was starving, thin and bony. My skin was dry and cracked, there were scabs on my lips, and my beard was long, tangled and dirty. No wonder the boy was frightened!

The pilot fought to gain control of the boat – in that turbulent sea, it was tossing about like a matchstick. He threw me a doubtful glance.

"Not if I can help it!" he shouted above the noise of the waves.

Then he concentrated on rowing the boat into smoother waters.

Chapter 6

At last, at long, long last, I felt land beneath my feet. And not just any land; it was my land, my home. I could hardly stand up straight – my knees were like jelly. The pilot grasped my arm to hold me up. His son still kept his distance, but the pilot chuckled.

"He's real enough," he said. "Skin and bone, it's true, but no ghost." Then he looked at me, and his gaze was troubled. "But as for those other creatures I saw on that ship of yours – well, I wouldn't be so sure. We'd better get you fed and watered, and I'm guessing a good night's sleep wouldn't go amiss. But after that – well, after that, it's as plain as the nose on my face that you've got a story to tell."

He glanced around. A crowd of people had gathered round us, curious and eager to help. "And I think I can say truly that every one of us wants to hear it!"

After I'd told them my story, I felt at peace. I felt just as I did when the albatross dropped from my neck: as if a terrible burden had fallen away from me.

And since then, I wander from land to land. I seem to have a strange power of speech. I see a particular man, and I know that he's the one I must tell my story to. Today, it was your face I saw. You were the one I had to tell.

He looked round. "There! You have a wedding to go to. I can hear all the voices. You'd better be on your way."

He smiled. He looked happy now. He looked as if he was at peace. "It's a beautiful world, isn't it? Look around you. Look at the trees. Look at the way the sun shines through the leaves. Look at how blue the sky is." Then he looked at me, and for an instant, his eyes glittered as they had when I first saw him. "Never forget how fortunate you are," he said fiercely.

I closed my eyes for a second, unable to bear the intensity of his gaze. When I opened them, he'd gone.

I didn't go to the wedding. I needed time alone, to think about the story I'd heard. What did it mean? Was it true?

I didn't know then, and I don't know now. But I do know I'll never forget that strange figure with the long grey beard and the glittering eyes. I'll never forget the Ancient Mariner.

The Ancient Mariner's Journey

remorse

guilt

release

fear

hope

despair

love

relief

Ideas for reading

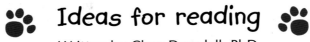

Written by Clare Dowdall, PhD
Lecturer and Primary Literacy Consultant

Reading objectives:

- discuss their understanding and explore the meaning of words in context
- draw inferences such as inferring characters' feelings, thoughts and motives from their actions, and justifying inferences with evidence
- predict what might happen from details stated and implied
- summarise the main ideas drawn from more than one paragraph, identifying key details that support the main ideas
- identify how language, structure and presentation contribute to meaning
- participate in discussions, presentations, performances, role play, improvisations and debates

Curriculum links: English – read a wide range of poetry

Resources: ICT, a copy of the poem *The Rime of the Ancient Mariner*, art materials for portrait drawing or painting

Build a context for reading

- Look at the front cover and read the title. Discuss the title and what an *Ancient Mariner* is. Challenge children to suggest synonyms for "ancient" and "mariner".
- Read the blurb together and share anything that is known about the famous poem, or the poet. Establish that this is a classic poem written nearly 300 years ago.
- Ask children to suggest what the Ancient Mariner might have been punished for, based on the blurb and the cover.

Understand and apply reading strategies

- Turn to pp2–4 and ask a volunteer to read the introduction aloud.
- Discuss how the characters are introduced and challenge children to find powerful descriptive words and phrases that describe the Ancient Mariner, e.g. "piercing", "merciless gaze".

Goodbye, we must be staying

'One, two, three, four…five!'
counted Reenie.
Alex and Zoe gasped. Above their
heads glowing corespore were
soaring up into the sky.
'Five corespore being carried off by
the five winds of Animalia,' sighed
Livingstone.
Alex thought for a minute.
'Five winds?'
The lion nodded. 'North, south, east,
west; and the Wind of No Return.'

Zoe shuddered. That last one
sounded strange.
The friends took a closer look at
the Core. It was bubbling angrily
and the colours were changing
every second.
'We need to get those corespore
back before there's trouble,'
frowned Livingstone.
Suddenly two more rocketed up
through the library skylight.

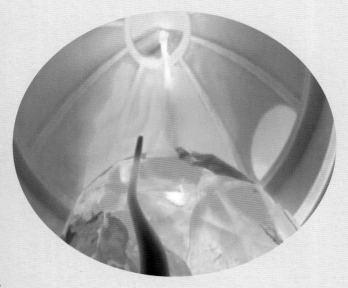

'Make that seven,' said Iggy, counting on his feet. 'I'm almost out of toes.'

Reenie put her head in her hooves. 'This is a disaster!'

Livingstone turned to Alex and Zoe as another two spore blasted out of the Core.

'The Core has great influence over Animalia, our lives and our language,' he explained. 'With nine Corespore missing, something will go wrong.'

Alex and G'Bubu knew what had to be done. Iggy scrambled up the gorilla's back as the team made their way out of the building.

'Let's find them before anything bad happens.'

'Let's roll!' shouted Alex. 'Zoe, are you coming?'
Zoe turned back towards the portal that had
brought them into Animalia. 'Actually, I was
thinking of going.'
Everybody stopped.
'I need to get back to reality,' she explained.
Alex's face fell. Iggy threw himself on to
the floor.
'Don't go Zoe! If you leave I will surely perish.'
      Zoe wriggled her nose. 'No you will not!'

G'Bubu caught Zoe's stare
with his big green eyes.
It was hard not to melt.
'Okay,' Zoe sighed.
'I'll stay... for a while.'

As the friends headed
out to search for the
nine corespore, a tenth
blazed through the
clouds above them.

Livingstone suddenly licked his lips.

'You know, Reenie,' he growled. 'I'm absolutely starving.'

But Reenie wasn't listening. She was watching the horrible hogs riding round the town square on their motorbikes.

'Their music is driving me crackers!' she barked. 'CHARGE!'

The rhino scraped her hooves then bolted after the shocked bikers.

'What's gotten into Reenie?' wondered Livingstone, as Fushia the Fox walked past.

For some reason, the lion couldn't help roaring at the delicious-looking creature.

'What's gotten into me?' cried Livingstone.

'Look down there!' cried Zed Zebra.

Zee peered over the side of the airship. 'Do you think they found one?'

Below them, G'Bubu, Alex and Zoe were dangling over the edge of a mountaintop. Iggy swung down to the bottom and plucked a corespore out of the cliff face.

The team had searched every corner of Animalia. They'd found corespore up trees and down caves. They had seven, but the last three were still out there somewhere.

Now they were back in the jungle.

'We've been searching for days,' groaned G'Bubu.

Alex looked through his binoculars. 'I saw something over there.'

And there it was. The eighth corespore was hanging from a branch in front of them. Everyone dashed towards it.

'AAAGGHGGHHHH!'

Suddenly they fell into a deep pit.
A fluttervision butterfly glided down
to the bottom of the pit. A picture
of Tyrannicus appeared on its wings.

'Stuck in a hole and can't get out? Call Tyrannicus' Towing Service,'
the tiger purred. 'Pay a fee and pick up the grapevine now!'

Iggy reached out for the vine hanging on the pit wall.

'Hello? Room service?'

The town square in Animalia had become a dangerous place to be.
The air was filled with the sound of howls and the squawks of terror.
Inside the library, Livingstone worked night and day on his research.
'Oh no, not those corespore…'
The books told him that the principles of Animalia itself were under
threat. The lion suddenly became aware of a snarling sound behind him.
'Reenie! Is that you?' he called out. 'I've figured out which corespore
are missing.'
Livingstone padded round the bookshelf, searching for his friend.
There, in a corner, he found a very angry rhinoceros.
'You're not Reenie,' he whispered.

Reenie snorted. Her eyes didn't even flicker as she hurled her great body towards the lion. 'Now if it's about that raise,' joked Livingstone. 'Can't we at least discuss it like civilised creatures?'

Reenie was in no mood for jokes. She chased the lion down the aisle, before he was forced to climb up a bookshelf to escape.

'Reenie!' Livingstone bellowed down. 'Cut that out!'

The rhino answered by ramming the shelf with her horn.

'It's all here Fushia,' beamed Tyrannicus. 'Give them a receipt.'

Zoe scowled. 'Sort of funny, don't you think? A fluttervision playing your ad at the bottom of that pit?'

'Plus a grapevine connected directly to your office?' added Alex.

Tyrannicus grinned. 'We aim to please.'

'You set that trap yourself!' shouted Zoe.

The tiger turned to his assistant. 'Come along Fushia, we have others in need who appreciate us.'

G'Bubu, Iggy, Zoe and Alex
made their way over to the
eighth corespore. Quick as a cat
Tyrannicus pounced.
'What have you got there?'
Alex held the orb to his chest.
'We need to get this back to
the Core.'
'I don't think so,' said
Tyrannnicus. 'I own the mineral
rights to this property.'

G'Bubu blocked the tiger's path.
Tyrannicus suddenly snarled and
drew out his claws.
'Give me the stone now!'
he roared.
'Boss, calm down,' soothed
Fushia. 'It's no big deal.'
Tyrannicus swiped at her,
eyes flashing with rage. The big
cat sank on to all fours,
then turned back to Alex and Zoe.

Snort! Crash! Thud!

Livingstone hung over the balcony, pleading with his librarian.

'Reenie! You can't come back inside until you promise to calm down!'

The rhino snorted then continued her attack on the library doors.

'You're going to pay for that door you know,' added Livingstone. He walked over to a window and gazed outside. Life as he knew it in Animalia had fallen apart.

'This is so much worse than I thought,' he said. 'They all look so wild, so… delicious.'

Livingstone gasped, shocked at what he'd just said. His savage roar echoed across the town square.

◆◆◆◆◆

'Come on!' screamed Alex. 'Keep going!'

The four friends pushed their way through the jungle, just one step ahead of Tyrannicus. The tiger bounded after them at frightening speed, determined to catch his prey.

'I am so glad I stayed now,' snapped Zoe. Being hunted by an angry tiger was a personal all-time low.

Alex pointed to a beam of white light in front of them.

'Quick! Into this portal, now!'

13

'What are you doin' in my kingdom?' bellowed Allegra.
G'Bubu and Iggy frowned. The portal must have sucked them in
and spat them out at Allegra's place.
'You mean the swamp?' G'Bubu asked.
'My swamp!' Allegra snapped.
Iggy noticed the tiara that the alligator was wearing.
'My fancy new crown makes me the ruler,' beamed Allegra. 'So git!'
G'Bubu stepped forward for a closer look. 'You say that thing is new?'
Zoe pointed up at the glowing gem. 'It's a corespore Allegra, you have
to hand that over!'

The alligator swished her tail. 'Over my stinkin' carcass! Never!' G'Bubu reached out, just missing the tiara.

'Help!' Allegra made a dash for it. 'They're trying to rob me of my royal sparkliness!'

Alex, Zoe and G'Bubu all ran after Allegra, before Iggy swung in and snatched the corespore off her head.

'That's mine!' she shrieked. The alligator began to hiss and clash her jaws. Alex paled as the reptile sunk to the ground, eyes darting from left to right. Alex and Zoe didn't need to say a word. It was time to be leaving.

Allegra chased the kids up to the Library. Zoe and Alex burst past Reenie, slamming the doors behind them.

As soon as everyone was inside, Alex tossed the first orb into the Core. It bounced off and clattered to the floor.
'We need to open them first!' yelled G'Bubu.
They began pulling and knocking the glowing stones. They were all locked.

'What do we do now?' said Alex.
'It's time to go!' whispered Zoe.
Iggy was standing next to the library computer. He pressed a button and pointed to a video recording of Animalia's ruler.
'Alex, Zoe, listen carefully. The ten missing corespore are from Animalia's Bill of Writes, which give our citizens the power of communication.'

Zoe tugged at Alex's sweatshirt. 'Let's leave now!'
As Alex tried to understand the lion's message, Zoe crept away to
the portal.
Livingstone's broadcast was interrupted by a loud roar.
'You need all ten corespore before you will be able to open any
of them. And if any were carried off by the Wind of No Return,
there's only one way to get them
back…'
'RrrooaaaaarrR!!'
Alex would have to watch
the recording later.

G'Bubu, Alex and Iggy were huddled together on top of a bookshelf. Down below, Livingstone paced up and down the library corridors.

'We are safe here,' whispered Iggy. 'And G'Bubu has packed a year's supply of bananas.'

On cue Livingstone leapt up to the ledge beside them. 'Cervantes!' squealed the lizard. 'I must evacuate myself immediately!'

The group jumped from shelf to shelf, toppling books in every direction. Livingstone was only a bite behind them. G'Bubu reached out an arm and swung Alex up to a window ledge.

Iggy looked over his shoulder as the trio headed back to the jungle. They were safe, for now…

———◆✕◆———

'Emma?' answered Zoe, back in her own dimension. 'I'm OK.
Have my parents been worried about me?'
She paused, then gaped at her mobile.
'What do you mean you just talked to me a minute ago?'
Zoe turned back towards the portal, but it was gone. Had nothing
really changed in the human world since she had visited Animalia?
It felt like she had been away for days.

———◆✕◆———

As soon as they could shake off Livingstone, Alex and G'Bubu rushed back to the Great Library. Iggy had disappeared.
A storm was raging inside the Core. 'That is definitely messed up,' muttered G'Bubu.
Alex rushed over to the wall where the portal back to the human world had been. There was nothing there. 'I'm glad that I have you to look out for me,' smiled Alex.

G'Bubu's friendly face suddenly twitched. The gorilla jumped on to his back feet and began beating his chest. Alex was on his own. Terrified, the boy backed towards the balcony railings. 'GGRRrrrrrrr!'
Alex turned to look over the balcony. Allegra, Livingstone and Tyrannicus were all waiting below, wild and threatening.

Zoe wandered along the library corridor. Something was telling
her not to go home yet.
'What's that?'
She felt a breeze circling her body, leading her towards the Weather
aisle. Zoe picked up a mysterious blue book.
She read the cover and gasped. ''The Wind of No Return'?'
There, tucked inside the book, was a corespore.
A passage of white light instantly flashed into being. It was Zoe's portal
back to Animalia!

The Core started to erupt.

Iggy ran towards Alex and G'Bubu, screeching with fear.

'At least we tried,' said Alex. His friends were wild now, but he sensed that at some level they might understand.

'Whoooaaa!'

Zoe tumbled into the Library.

'Look what I found!' she cried. 'Compliments of the Wind of No Return.'

Alex beamed. 'The tenth corespore!'

The pair raced towards the Core. As soon as Alex held up the blue spore, it opened. The room hushed as a bird with turquoise wings flew out and hovered in front of them. It sung a message before soaring away. 'Words can change your life.'

All of the other glowing eggs opened, releasing nine more birds.
'Writing is a window to your mind,' chanted one.
'Be careful what you say and how you say it!' cried another.
As the birds disappeared into the very top of the Core, it
suddenly calmed.
G'Bubu and Iggy rushed up to Alex and Zoe, pulling them into a hug.
'I'm glad that's over.'
The friends spun round to see Livingstone, back to his normal self.
Allegra and Tyrannicus were right behind him too.
'Bang-a-lang!' squealed Allegra. 'What am I doing here?'

'We are no longer hissing monsters!' laughed Iggy. 'This is good.'
G'Bubu nodded. 'Dude! Dudette! You saved us!'
'And you saved Animalia too,' added Livingstone.
Alex looked back at the white light flickering in the corner.
'Found your own portal I see.'
Zoe smiled. 'Yep. I guess Animalia is not just your thing after all.'
The pair turned to greet the crowd of creatures waiting on the library
steps. Zebras, hogs and foxes all wanted to shake their hands.
Alex looked at Zoe and grinned. 'Glad to be back?'
'Very.'